SPLITS AND GIGGLES

SPLITS AND GIGGLES

37 Years of Owning a Bowling Alley

JOSEPH E. SCHWARZEL

PALMETTO
PUBLISHING
Charleston, SC
www.PalmettoPublishing.com

Copyright © 2024 by Joseph E. Schwarzel

All rights reserved

No portion of this book may be reproduced, stored in a retrieval system, or transmitted in any form by any means-electronic, mechanical, photocopy, recording, or other-except for brief quotations in printed reviews, without prior permission of the author.

Paperback ISBN: 979-8-8229-4863-1

TABLE OF CONTENTS

Preface··vii
Acknowledgments··65

PREFACE

It is important to read this introduction to understand what I'm trying to explain about what it's been like to own a bowling center for thirty-seven years. Hello—my name is Joseph E. Schwarzel. I was born in January 1949 in a small town called Rodi, Pennsylvania, which is now known as Penn Hills. In October 1950 we moved out into the country to a small town called Murrysville. In 1966 I graduated from Franklin Regional High School, where I set a school record of seventy-eight games of tennis in one day. That record is still standing to this day.

I learned a lot of my work ethic in Murrysville: working in a body shop when I was thirteen years old, cooking hamburgers in a fast-food restaurant for eighty-five cents per hour, landscaping, and pumping gas with a walking cast on my right foot after surgery. While landscaping, I met a man who was the head of industrial relations at Westinghouse. He told me to give him a call if I ever wanted a job at Westinghouse, which I did, and I was hired almost immediately. Six months later I was tested for the maintenance apprenticeship, which I know I didn't pass, but it's nice to know people in high places.

Most of the episodes in this book are as exact as I can remember; however, sometimes I have a tendency to slightly exaggerate.

Sometime around Thanksgiving of 1975, my wife, Polly, came home to our apartment in Level Green. She had been bowling in a traveling league that night. She proceeded to tell me that a bowling alley was for sale.

The next few days went by as usual. She went to work as a draftsman, and I went to work as a carpenter—both at Westinghouse but in different plants: she was at Forest Hills, and I was at East Pittsburgh. As time went on, she started dropping hints such as "I always wanted to own a bowling alley—my dad managed a bowling alley in Greensburg. You can make a lot of money in a bowling alley." Then she dropped the big hammer on me when she said, "There's a lot of maintenance to owning a bowling alley." That was it.

She knew I was a four-year-course graduate apprentice in maintenance at Westinghouse.

We then started discussing the situation with her parents, Bob and Pavline. Her dad said, "Why don't you call and see what they want for the place?" The next day the phone call was made: $250,000 with a $50,000 deposit would buy it. Now the gears started turning. Where were we going to get that kind of money?

My wife and I had saved about $8,000. Bob and Pavline could sell their house for $38,000. We'd still be $4,000 short, so I went to the credit union at work to see if I could borrow $4,000. "No problem," said John L., one of the credit union officers.

Next step: let's go look at this place. Following my wife's directions, I started wondering where in the hell she was taking me. It was a winding road, up and down hills, until suddenly I somehow recognized a tunnel where you had to stop and blow your horn. I remembered my grandfather hauling coal out of this town when I was only five years old. On we went up a long, winding road to the location.

When we pulled into what looked like a parking lot, I was shocked. A dilapidated-looking building with peeling paint and soffit boards falling off—what a mess. Oh well, let's go inside and take a look. When we entered, there was a youngster bowling with a chair in the middle of the lane. He was trying to make his ball roll between the legs of the chair, but with no luck—bang, bang, bang! The chair went flying.

As we looked around, we could obviously see that the place was in bad need of a good maintenance man—guess who.

After a lengthy conversation with the owner, we told him we would talk it over and let him know in a week or so. To make a long story short, we decided to buy the place. After all the legal BS was over, the moving process began. My wife and I moved out of our apartment and into a sixty-foot-by-twelve-foot mobile home as the formal owners in the second week of April 1976. Weeks passed, and shortly thereafter my in-laws moved into the same trailer. My wife, her mom, dad, brother, and I all in the same trailer—and oh yes, a small poodle named Michele.

Now the former owner had us between a rock and a hard place. He informed us he had twelve more lanes stashed at different locations and wanted to know if we would be interested in adding on to the existing eight lanes. The negotiations began. We decided to have him draw up the plans, and we would take a look at them. The plans included twelve additional lanes, restrooms, a utility room, and a seventy-five-foot-square basement. It looked good to us—how much more money?

Splits and Giggles

The price went from $250,000 to $375,000, which we agreed to. Construction began quickly, with the former owner in charge. The footer was poured, blocks were laid, and everything was going well until one day, while laying the block in the basement area, the former owner decided to backfill the rear wall against the block layers' advice. Two-thirds of the rear wall collapsed: pea gravel, rebar, wire mesh. What a mess.

We were ready to open. Finally, from that day on, construction went fairly well until late in August, when through the door came a ladies' league scheduled to start bowling. No one told us they were to start that night. We didn't have the restrooms done yet! Luckily, my elder brother came to visit that night. We quickly set a toilet, hung a sink, and put up a temporary curtain. The ladies started bowling, and would you believe a pinsetter broke down? I called the former owner to see if he would show me how to fix it. His reply was "I can't be coming down every time a machine breaks down," and he hung up. Then another machine broke down. I called my wife to come help.

When she got there, I said, "Sit here and feed the pins in by hand while I try to fix the second machine." We both sat on those machines until the end of the night. I looked over at her and thought, What in the hell did you get me into?

The following Friday night was another surprise: the Friday-night men's league started—once again no one informed us. Everything was going smoothly until disaster struck. A bolt fell out of the pin deck light, and the rake caught it, shattering the fluorescent light all over lanes 2, 3, and 4. How embarrassing. Play had to be stopped until we cleaned up the mess and repaired the light. Later that evening one of the bowlers brought his ball to the counter, saying it was getting nicked up. I told him to leave it when he was finished, and I would fix it. When he brought it down at the end of the night, I noticed all the marks were in the same spot, about fifteen of them—you could cover them with a quarter. I asked, "Tommy, what line are you playing?" His reply was "Second arrow." At the end of the night, I got on my hands and knees on the lane, and sure enough, on the second arrow was a piece of glass from the light breaking, embedded in the lane. How accurate a bowler was that guy?

Lane 3 seemed to be the jinx lane of the house. I came home from work one day, sat down at the supper table, and noticed an unusual silence between my wife and mother-in-law. I didn't say anything for a few minutes. When I couldn't stand it any longer, I said, "What's wrong?" The look I got from my wife was priceless. She said the roof was caving in over lane 3. Luckily, Uncle Paul was there and propped it up temporarily. Uncle Paul was a very knowledgeable construction worker. He and I discussed what we were going to do with the situation. I told him if he could find three or four two-by-eight boards twenty feet long, I could borrow a banding machine from work. Lucky for me the next day was Friday. I went to my boss to see if I could borrow the banding machine for the weekend, and he said it was no problem. That weekend was spent jacking the rafters back into place, scabbing the new twenty-foot boards to the existing rafters, and banding them together with the steel straps. It was quite a project for the two of us, but we got it done.

The next adventure on lane 3 was when Rodney came to me and said, "Can you get my ball out of the ceiling?"

My look of doubt to him made him laugh. I said, "How did your ball get in the ceiling?"

He said, "My thumb stuck, and it went up in the ceiling."

So up we went to lane 3. There was no evidence of a ball hitting the ceiling tile or anything unusual. I walked down the capping between lanes 3 and 4, picked up a ceiling tile, and lo and behold there lay a bowling ball. He hit the tile so perfectly he knocked it up in the air, and it came down perfectly back in place. The next line I saw Rodney doing was not on a bowling lane but rather in the men's room. As I entered the men's room, he and a friend were doing a line of coke on the sink. I said, "Get that shit out of here." They both left. Two weeks later he returned to thank me for getting him off that crap.

The next interesting thing in the men's room was when I had just finished mopping the floor, and fifteen minutes later someone told me someone had pissed on the floor. I remopped the floor and took a look in the poolroom to see who was there: two regular boys shooting pool and a stranger with long blond hair and a thin build. The day went by as usual until around 1:00 p.m., when once again I was told about the same problem. I took another look in the poolroom—several different regulars but same young boy with long blond hair. I had just eaten supper around 5:00 p.m. and went to relieve Bob so he could eat. Well, guess who I passed going to the restroom as he entered. I waited a couple of seconds, and as I opened the restroom door, guess who was standing there pissing on the wall. I grabbed him by the back of his collar and the back of his belt, and out we went to the front door. Bob's mouth dropped open when he saw me throw someone out that way. I later found out from the school kids he was being raised by a single mother, and his dad was in the service at the time. I was also told he was using quaaludes at that time.

The poolroom consisted of two four-foot-by-eight-foot pool tables, several pinball machines, and some very new things called video machines. As I remember, *Crazy Climber* and *Pong* were some of the earliest games, followed by *Donkey Kong* and several others. We had a great group of kids who really appreciated what we were doing for them. There wasn't much more to do in the township. I started shooting pool with many of them, getting to know them by name. Several of them became friends, not just customers. However, every once in a while, you would get a bad kid in there. I was informed that someone was spitting on the floor between two pinball machines. I casually walked into the room, and just as I was behind some young boy, he spat on the floor. I grabbed him by the shoulders and spun him around. I asked, "Do you spit on the floor at home?" He said no, so I replied, "Well, this is my home. Get out."

Later that evening the young boy returned with his big brother. They stopped just inside the door and motioned me to come over, which I did. The big brother said to me, "Are you the one that grabbed my brother earlier today?"

I replied, "Yes—he was spitting on the floor."

He said, "Are you going to grab me if I spit on the floor?"

I replied yes. He started to tremble, then turned and left the building. I was glad because he was a pretty big boy.

In the early days of DLB, it seemed like everyone wanted a new ball drilled. I wasn't familiar with how to drill a ball, so I practiced on several house balls until some of them looked like Swiss cheese.

The drilling machine looked like something Columbus had brought with him on the boat. Seven feet tall and made of cast iron, it had a three-inch-wide leather belt driven by a jig, designed to drill bowling balls. One of the most challenging drillings I ever did was for a 172-average bowler who had lost his thumb in a waterskiing accident. After experimenting on several house balls, we finally drilled a ball he could grip. He ended up bowling close to his average.

I was then approached by a lady who wanted me to drill a ball the same as her old ball. She said, "Can you match it perfectly?"

I replied, "I'll do my best." She told me she was going to a tournament in Monroeville, a suburb of Pittsburgh, where the first place was worth $1,000. The following weekend the tournament was over, and she was in first place. However, when she threw her last ball, the tournament director confiscated it and said it was illegal because the weight was wrong. She would have to leave it there to have it checked. When she returned and told me that, I was sick. I didn't need a reputation for drilling illegal balls. A week went by before she was told everything was OK, and she won the $1,000. What a relief to me.

Bobby was pretty much in charge of lane maintenance, which included dusting caps and gutters, back pushing, and reoiling the lanes. One day he informed me that someone must be lofting their ball way out on the lane because he was seeing huge dents in the soft pine boards. The way a bowling lane is built, the boards from the foul line are made of laminated maple. A hardwood to fifteen feet out on the lane then turns to laminated pine board, which is a much softer wood. When a ball is lofted out past the hardwood and lands on the much softer pine board, it leaves a dent in the lane, much like a pothole on a road. Well, it turns out that the following Friday night Bobby was bowling in the Friday-night men's league. He observed another team's members trying to convince one of their members to see how far he could loft the ball. As you may have guessed, alcohol was heavily involved. After he heaved the ball twenty-two to twenty-five feet down the lane, which resounded with a heavy thud, his teammates roared. He was shortly escorted out of the lanes by the police department.

At the end of the night, Bobby told me who the person was. I was not surprised, but I knew where his locker was and what kind of ball he threw. The ball he threw was a popular one at the time, featuring a cork-impregnated core. I knew that type of core would be porous and would absorb fluid, such as WD-40—a penetrating fluid and very slippery. I was pissed about the way he was destroying the lanes, so I set his ball in the locker with the thumb hole up and filled it with the WD-40. The next day I checked the ball, and sure enough the fluid was absorbed into the core. So I filled it again! The next Friday night came, and sure enough, in the third game, after numerous beers, his teammates started again to urge him to see how far he could loft the ball. Someone heard him say, "My thumb is so slippery I can't even hold on to the ball." Guess why. I took care of that problem, didn't I!

There is never a dull moment in the bowling industry. One day my brother, one of the regular bowlers and a good friend named Curt, and I were doing some roof work. We had just come off the roof and were sitting in the front yard, having a well-deserved beer, when all of a sudden, we heard my neighbor yell to his wife, "Call the fire department! The house is on fire!" It turned out they had just moved into the house, and he was soldering in the laundry room and caught the insulation on fire. Across East Union Road I ran, with Curt right behind. Brother John ran for a fire extinguisher. As I entered the front door, the smoke was coming up from the cellar steps. I immediately grabbed something out of the laundry basket—God only knows what it was—and told Curt, "Get something so you can breathe!" I was pulling the burning insulation out of the wall and handing it to Curt to get it outside. The next thing I remember is sitting in the grass with an oxygen mask on, being asked if I was OK. I said, "I swallowed a lot of smoke," but being a former firefighter, I knew I was OK. After calm had resumed, Curt said, "I wouldn't follow just anyone into a burning building, but I'd follow you anytime."

The bowling industry is an unusual business. If you don't keep up with the Joneses, you have to close the door. So we decided to update by changing the masking units. The masking units are the false walls in front of the pinsetters. The ones we had were from the late '50s. Four of the ones on the new side, lanes 9–20, were, for some reason, from Japan. When we lit them up, they looked like a Japanese Fourth of July. Lanes 17–20 did not match lanes 9–16. I ended up cutting over three hundred feet of wires and lights out of them. It wasn't long before some idiot threw a ball so hard it jumped out of the gutter and blew a huge hole in one of them. I tried to glue it back together, but it looked like shit. Next, we decided to go with a jet-black package that included an accelerator to get the ball back to the bowler quicker and speed up play—I was all for that. It also came with new masking units, complete with first- and second-ball lights and a strike-light X for every time a strike was thrown. New phenolic decks were also installed, eliminating our old pin decks, which were in bad shape.

As the weeks and years rolled on, many funny, serious, and interesting events happened. A bowler came in for a second-shift league on a Wednesday night and said there was a fight in the parking lot. Very unusual, I thought, but I'd better investigate. As I went out the door, I went flat on my back because of the freezing rain. The fight turned out to be two ladies who were rolling on the ice and couldn't get up. I tried to help them up, but the ice was too slippery. I said, "I'll be right back!"

As I ran past Bob, he said, "Where are you going?"

I said, "To put my golf spikes on!" He looked bewildered.

I returned to the foyer, golf shoes in hand. Even when I had the golf spikes on, the ice was no match for me. I got to the ladies. I said to Terri, "Let's get you up first. Then you can help me get Brenda up." They were both laughing so hard they pissed themselves. I helped them to their cars, and away they went.

On a Sunday afternoon, one of our regular bowlers said, "Bob, can I get a beer?"

Bob said, "Sure, thirty-five cents." We had a refrigerator in the utility room. Thirty-five cents for a beer—can you believe that? We weren't making any money selling beer; we were doing it as a public service.

There was a gentleman bowling on lane 20. He approached Bob and said, "I just saw that man get a beer. Could I get one?"

Bob, being the nice guy that he was, said, "Sure, thirty-five cents."

I said, "Bob, you don't know that guy. What if he's LCB?" Bob just shrugged. Guess what he was!

The following Monday Bob made a beer run for the league bowlers in his old brown Ford van. I unloaded twenty-five cases of beer behind lane 9. When the phone rang down at the trailer, Bob said, "We're being raided by the LCB." I hurried behind lane 9 and threw twenty-five cases out the back door so they didn't get them. They did, however, get our half barrel out of the refrigerator, plus three or four cases.

Senior citizens are some of my favorite people. When you talk to them, you never know what kind of a story you might hear. But once in a while, one of them does something out of the ordinary. John C., who owned a car dealership in the area but was now retired, loved to bowl. One Sunday afternoon he came in to practice, as he often did. He was bowling on lane 18 when a pin slid off to a spot where the pinsetter couldn't pick it up. The deck came down on top of the pin and stopped, just as it is designed to do. When that happens, I have to go behind the pinsetter and manually pull a rod called the out-of-range rod, and the pinsetter will continue to cycle, and the bowler can finish the frame. Well, John apparently decided to fix the machine himself. He started walking down the lane and was halfway down to the pinsetter when I yelled at him and said, "John, stop! I'll get that for you!" I proposed to fix the machine and came out to see what he was going to do.

He said, "I was just going to kick it out of the way."

I said, "John, if you would have done that, that deck weighs 284 pounds and would have stopped eleven-sixteenths of an inch above the deck and would have probably broken your leg." He just chuckled and continued to bowl.

Another senior named Ben was interesting—he was one of the very few Black bowlers in our establishment. He was quite a character, always busting my stones about something. One day he called on the phone—I recognized his voice. He said, "Did you find my satchel?" I didn't know what a satchel was, but I told him I'd found a lady's purse.

Splits and Giggles

An hour later he came in and said, "Let me see that purse you found." I showed him what I thought was a lady's purse. His eyes got really big and said, "That's my satchel." He must have thanked me a dozen times and left. I didn't know at the time, but in his satchel was $3,500 to $4,000 worth of photography equipment. The next time he came in, he took several pictures of me, for reasons I didn't know. Two weeks later he presented me with a beautiful sweatshirt and T-shirt with my picture on it and a caption "Honest Abe at work." Then came the day he was bowling, and his hip went out of place. He was in excruciating pain. I called an ambulance, then I called his son.

The next time I saw Ben was in a local store. He had a lady friend with him and immediately started busting my stones. He introduced his lady friend to me, and I said, "Nice to meet you. Have you known Ben very long?"

She replied, "Oh yes, a long time."

I said, "You have my sympathy." She laughed until tears ran down her cheeks.

The next senior I had to deal with was Nick D. Nick was a veteran of the Korean War. In my opinion he was a rather strange person. Every time he came in, he would relate to me a different episode of his life. One day he told me that before he went to sleep at night, he had to lock all the windows in his house. I asked, "Why do you do that, Nick?"

He said, "So I don't jump out of them." He then told me he had to lock up all the knives and sharp objects so he didn't hurt himself in the middle of the night.

One day he saw my dog, a black lab, come into the lanes. He said, "You don't see dogs in Korea."

I said, "Why is that, Nick?"

His reply was "They eat them."

Nick always had a sheepish grin on his face. You never knew if he was smiling at you or going to do something absurd behind your back. Nick joined the Monday-night men's league, usually a very calm league. One night things started getting a little out of control, so I listened a little closer. Back in those days, score keeping was done on a paper score sheet; automatic scoring and telescores were not yet being used. According to the score sheet, Nick had missed a spare in the previous frame. When Nick got up to bowl the next frame, he noticed the open frame. He said, "I made that spare," and an argument started, escalating rapidly. Things got louder and louder until Nick said, "Next week I'll bring a gun and kill all you assholes!" He literally threw his ball into his bag and stormed out of the lanes. Now what did I do? Did I notify the police, or should I just handle the situation myself?

It just so happened that one of the township police officers bowled here, so I asked him what I should do. He said, "Observe him closely, and if he looks nervous, notify the police."

The following Monday came, and here came Nick, carrying his bowling bag. His shirt was tucked into his pants, so I couldn't see any unusual bulges. I watched as he took his ball out of the bag and placed it on the rack. I waited for the right moment and causally looked in his bowling bag—no gun. What a relief.

The next senior situation was a sad one. Liz M. bowled in the Monday-night ladies' league, and her husband, Lou, bowled in the Monday-night men's league. Lou was a very large man with the temperament of a teddy bear. Liz was the sweetest little old lady you would ever want to meet. Unfortunately Lou became ill and went to the great beyond. As in many cases like this, Liz felt very lonely and went through a long mourning situation that lasted almost two years. Then one Sunday afternoon, she came into the lanes with a new companion named Ed. After the hugs and introductions, I gave them lane 8, on the upper section of the lanes. Partway into the second game, I heard an unusual thump. When I turned and looked, I saw Liz lying on the approach with her legs splayed in different directions. I hurried to her aid and said, "Liz, don't move." She started to apologize for throwing her ball into the wall, and I said, "Don't worry about that." It turned out that when she picked her ball up off the ball rack, her hip broke, causing her to throw the ball into the wall. She asked me to take her shoes off, and I said, "I'll take one off, but I'll let the paramedics do the other one." That was the last time I ever saw Liz.

Next, a tall, lanky senior came through the door, carrying a new ball in a box in one hand and an old, beat-up ball on his shoulder like a shot in shot put. His name was Bill B. I knew who he was, but I'd never met him personally. His wife bowled in the Wednesday-night ladies' league. He wouldn't bowl here because of a previous altercation with the former owner. He began by showing me his old ball and giving me the history of it, telling me how it got chewed up at another establishment. Next, he said, "I hear you are pretty good at drilling bowling balls."

I said, "I've done quite a few."

He said, "I throw a backup ball. Can you match my old ball perfectly?"

I said, "I'll give it a try. You'll have to leave it here because I'm here by myself. You can pick it up on Tuesday."

He said, "That's great—I bowl Tuesday night." On Wednesday afternoon he stormed through the door like a mad hornet. He jumped all over me, saying, "I told you I threw a backup ball! This ball won't back up!"

I told him, "Bill, these new balls have weight blocks in them. Your old ball didn't have them." I said, "That ball will still back up."

He said, "No way. I'll give you ten thousand bucks if you can make it back up."

I turned on lane 8, and he followed me up the steps to watch. When I threw the ball, I twisted my wrist, and lo and behold the ball backed up. He said, "I'll be damned," and reached for his wallet.

I said, "I don't want your money, Bill." He grabbed his ball, and I never saw him again.

Once in a while, we would encounter a bad customer and had to pick them out quickly. They would spill pop and not tell us, not put their pool sticks back in the rack, and try to get extra time on the pool table. One Sunday night he called, and I recognized his voice. He said, "There is a bomb in the lanes set to go off at 8:00," and told me to evacuate the building.

When I hung up the phone, I told Bob, "We just got a bomb threat."

He said, "What are we going to do? We have twenty lanes going. Should we notify the police?"

I said, "No, I know who made that call, and he hasn't been in here tonight, but just to be safe, I'll check all the obvious places—garbage cans, restrooms, and so on." Now I was watching the clock. At 7:55 p.m., I walked out into the parking lot, and guess who was sitting there waiting for the evacuation. I approached him and said that the police had been notified and that he had better knock that shit off. I then found out his family had moved out of the township.

The next prank phone call asked if we had eight-pound balls. "Of course," we would reply.

"How in the hell do you hold them up?" would be the question, followed by some young girls giggling.

After thirty or forty of these calls, I started playing their silly game. I would reply, "We have black balls, red balls, green balls, and a trace on this phone call—the police will be notifying you very soon." That was the end of the prank calls.

Splits and Giggles

Sunday nights were quite laid-back nights: a couples' league on lanes 9–20 in the lower section and a men's church league on lanes 1–8 in the upper section. During the ten-minute practice session, I noticed a grubby-looking person coming through the door, obviously not a bowler. He headed straight for the upper section, particularly to a person named Shawn. I immediately sensed trouble. I cautiously watched until it was time for me to intervene. As I approached him, it was obvious he was visibly intoxicated. I said, "I need to see you downstairs right now!" He followed me into the utility room, and I closed the door.

He began by saying "He owes me money."

I said, "I don't care what's between you and Shawn, but in that league are Shawn's dad, his brother, a magistrate, a state police officer, and an Allegheny County sheriff. I don't think you want to go up against those odds. I suggest you leave." And away he went.

We needed a liquor license—that's all there was to it! Time after time people carrying in coolers would ask us, "When are you going to get a license?" So we started investigating. We were told that the township already had too many licenses per capita, so the only way we could get one was to buy an existing license that was for sale. Alas, we found out that a little old lady in Russellton wanted to sell her license. We jumped at the chance and bought it. Now transferring the license a mile up over the hill became a different problem. After several attempts to transfer the license, we were denied by the township for various reasons: too close to the church, noise problems, not properly zoned—that did it! "Not properly zoned," said the letter from Harrisburg signed by the township zoning officer. When I saw this refusal, I blew my top. I went to the municipal building with my wife and both daughters, the letter in one hand and my youngest daughter in the other. I confronted the zoning officer in this manner: "You falsified this information on purpose about our zoning being R-1 instead of C-1," and I called to his attention the seven-foot-by-five-foot map hanging behind his chair on the wall, with our property highlighted in red.

By now the police officer on duty must have heard my overzealous voice and said, "What's going on in here?"

I held out the letter and said, "This man falsified information to Harrisburg about our zoning. I have a notion to sue this township."

The zoning officer said I must have made a mistake. Well, the mistake he made was handed over to our attorney, Jake O. This must have pissed off Jake to no end. He told us to gather up all the correspondence between us and the township, which we did and delivered it to him. The next time the township had a supervisors' meeting, guess who was in attendance: the cool, suave, debonaire man-about-town, Jake, in a three-piece-suit and tie, looking like a high-priced attorney with all the letters in hand. To say he read the riot act to the supervisors would be putting it mildly. He informed them that we had every right to sue the township. A letter of apology was sent to us by the township. The next step was a hearing with the Pennsylvania Liquor Control Board in Carnegie, a suburb of Pittsburgh. When we showed up at the hearing, we had a busload of people all in favor of us having a liquor license. The presiding judge at the hearing said he'd never heard of a busload of people in favor of a liquor license; it's usually the other way around. The hearing was in our favor, and we were granted the license. Next came the converting of the poolroom into a bar, which meant adding on to the existing building for a kitchen, a storage room, restrooms, and coolers. The construction moved along quickly with aid from relatives and several very helpful friends.

Speaking of construction, it seems like a never-ending process in this industry. The new twelve lanes had subway ball returns and telescores. The old eight lanes upstairs still had above-lane ball returns, and bowlers had to keep score with a pencil and paper. We got a lot of complaints. So we contacted a well-known bowling contractor from Pittsburgh named Dick. He came out for a meeting, and we talked about putting in subway ball returns. One thing led to another. The eight lanes upstairs were built on two different elevations. Lanes 1–4 were eight inches higher than lanes 5–8, which I always thought was stupid construction. The whole upstairs had a flat roof with eight different elevations, which was nothing but problems. The more we talked, the more we both had suggestions and remedies.

I said, "How much is this going to cost?"

"Forty-four thousand," Dick replied.

Being familiar with construction, I said, "That sounds fair. When do we start?" Then the light went on in my head. Dick had said he would have to jackhammer the concrete between each pair of lanes, build forms, and pour concrete. I said, "What if we raised lanes 5 through 8 to the same level as 1 through 4?" He said that would save him lots of work, and he had four Brunswick lanes in his warehouse that would match lanes 1–4. Lanes 5–8 were AMF lanes for some reason. Then he said he had telescore units that would match lanes 9–20. I said, "Wait a minute! We're going to put subway ball returns on lanes 1 through 8, Brunswick lanes to match 1 through 4, telescores to match lanes 9 through 20—the whole place is going to look the same?"

He said, "Absolutely."

I said, "What's the difference in price?"

He said, "Same price: forty-four thousand." He added, "You'll be helping me by getting my warehouse cleaned out."

Then this construction would present another problem. For the telescores to work, we would have to raise the ceiling above the approach area. Fortunately, one of the bowlers on Friday night had a construction company, and he gave us a bid that we couldn't refuse. I don't remember what year it was, but it was somewhere in the early '80s. Everything went fairly well, and when the bowlers came in the next fall, they were surprised. I always said walking into the lanes was like walking into a big box of Cracker Jack. You never knew what the surprise was going to be.

One Saturday afternoon I went into the lounge area and saw a grubby person. I knew who he was. His grandma told my mother-in-law his family had disowned him, although he came from a very well-known family. He was throwing darts at the dart machine—not putting money in, just throwing darts. I said to the bartender, "What's he drinking?"

"Water" was her reply.

My thought was, Anything free. A few minutes later, I returned and said, "Did he leave?"

"No," she replied, "but I wish he would. He's creepy, and he keeps staring at me."

I said, "Where is he?"

She said, "In the men's room. He's been in there a long time."

I thought I'd better see what he was up to. When I opened the door, there stood Ray stark-ass naked, with wet paper towels all over the floor. His socks and underwear were draped on the sink, looking as if they might have been white at one time. I said, "What do you think you're doing?"

He said, "I haven't had a f****ing bath in a month."

I said, "Get dressed and get the f**k out of here! If I see you on my property again, I'll have you arrested for trespassing!" I never saw him again.

We had several different cleaning personnel, but one was a little old lady named Peggy. She was very short, not even five feet tall, and she took eight-inch steps, which made it take her forever to clean. One Tuesday morning I was fixing a high nail in the channel on lane 7 that was damaging balls. Peggy came out of the lounge and yelled, "Joe! This man is a state trooper and wants to talk to you!"

I said, "Yes, sir, how can I help you?"

He said, "I need to see your liquor license, your liquor bottles, and all your receipts from the liquor store."

I said, "Do you mind telling me what this is about?"

He repeated, "I need to see your liquor license, your liquor bottles, and all your receipts from the liquor store."

I thought, Wow, this guy is serious! I walked him into the lounge and said, "There is the license."

He said, "That's supposed to be in a glass frame."

I said, "The cleaning lady knocked it off the wall last week and broke the glass. I'll have it fixed today. There are the liquor bottles." I pointed to the speed rack.

He picked up every bottle and examined it. He said, "Where are the receipts?"

I said, "They're in the office downstairs." He followed me down to the office, where my wife sat. I said to her, "Hon, this man is a state police officer. He needs to see the receipts from the liquor store." I said, "They're in the file cabinet, in a folder marked 'state store' or 'liquor store,' I'm not sure." She handed him the folder, and he looked at every receipt.

He said, "You folks aren't doing anything wrong. This place is too clean."

Once again I said, "Can you tell me what this is about?"

He said, "You've been turned in for watering down your liquor bottles."

I chuckled, and he glared at me. I said, "That's about the stupidest thing you can do as a bar owner." It was probably Linda—I had caught her stealing from me, and I fired her on the spot. On her way out the door, she threatened to turn me in for everything, whatever that was.

The state trooper thanked me for being so cooperative and said he was never greeted with "How can I help you?"

In the early '80s, we had a large ladies' league—sixty ladies, three on a team. They took all twenty lanes. I was having electrical problems on lane 18; it kept blowing fuses. Halfway through the third game, my last spare fuse blew. I did something stupid: I spliced two wires together just to get through the night. About six or eight minutes later, one of the ladies, named Cindy, came running back to the counter and said, "That machine is on fire." By the time I got to the machine, the entire electrical box was in flames, which I quickly extinguished. We had to move them to the next pair of lanes.

When we first bought the place, Bobby had two teenage helpers, Jeff and Bill. They were helping move some spare parts into the basement. Like two rambunctious teens, they were always horsing around. Lane 9 burned up a solenoid and needed to have it replaced. I knew I had a spare one but couldn't find it. I looked for that spare solenoid for three days but couldn't find it anywhere and thought maybe it got put in the basement. I went down to look—no solenoid. The next day guess who came through the door: Jeff and Bill—they always hung around together. I asked if they had seen the solenoid. They both said at the same time, "What's a solenoid?" So I described it to them: a two-inch square with a hole in it, attached to a three-inch piece of electrical cord with a plug on the end. They looked at each other and started to laugh and said, "I bet it's that thing we threw in the woods."

I said, "I need it. Go find it." Ten minutes later the solenoid was lying on the counter.

On Wednesday night I golfed in a league in Murrysville, where I grew up. A lot of the guys I went to school with also golfed in that league. Sometimes we would get together at the Export Moose and talk about old times and naturally have a few beers. One night I stayed there longer than I should have. My wife was more than a little bit ticked off at me. She informed me the police were at the bowling center because one of the bowlers had her car stolen out of our parking lot. I said, "Whose was it?"

"Nancy's" was her reply.

Nancy was a girl who, in my opinion, thought she was God's gift to men. She was a blonde with buckteeth. Nancy was a bit different from most girls at that time in that she had restored a Pontiac GTO that she owned. I never saw the car, but I was told she did a pretty good job restoring it. The following Wednesday I came straight home after golf. When Nancy came in, she jumped all over me for not having better security in the parking lot. Nancy didn't know, but I had inside information that they'd found her car out on a gas line on Rich Hill Road with the keys still in it. I said, "Nancy, you shouldn't have left the keys in it, or it wouldn't have been stolen."

She said, "I was in a hurry."

I said, "You had to turn the car off. You should have pulled the keys out."

She said, "I always leave my key in the car. You need better security."

My grandfather always said, "Don't argue with someone dumber than yourself. You'll never learn anything."

On Christmas night I'd just gotten home from visiting my dad in Rodi, Pennsylvania, which is now called Penn Hills. I said to my wife, "I'm going up to the lanes to do a walk-around," which involved checking the doors and lights and seeing if anything is wrong. I'd no sooner opened the door than it sounded like someone was running a jackhammer. I turned on the lights, and OMG, water was pouring down from the ceiling into outer lanes 6, 7, and 8. I knew there was no waterline there that could have broken. What the heck was going on? I called down to the house and said, "Get up here. I need help now." It turned out we'd had a terrific ice storm that week, and water couldn't get to the gutters. A roof vent had been removed during previous construction and was acting like a chimney. I got into the crawl space with one-inch Styrofoam, a plastic bag, and a roll of duct tape. Lanes 6, 7, and 8 were badly damaged. I finally got to bed around 4:00 a.m.

When we first bought the lanes, the twenty-foot-by-forty-foot swimming pool in the front yard had no fence around it. I don't know how he ever got away with the zoning laws about that. One morning, about five o'clock, I was awakened by a god-awful howling noise. When I opened the door, there was a collie swimming in the pool exhausted, giving his death howl. I reached in and grabbed him by the back of his neck and pulled him out. I was going to kick him for waking me up, but I figured he had been through enough.

During a time of heavy construction, we were installing synthetic lanes over the old wooden ones. The synthetics came in fifteen-foot sections, seven-sixteenths of an inch thick, made of a very dense material. Each panel weighed forty-five to fifty pounds. We had bundles of panels stacked throughout the bowling center. One of the installers was named Curtis. He was a Southern boy from Tennessee, huskily built—strong as a bull. I didn't see what happened, but Curtis said to me, "That boy hit the ground hard." It was a Saturday night, a couples' league bowling—usually a quiet night. I asked Curtis what happened. He said, "That boy right there threw that blond boy on the ground real hard."

He pointed to a guy named Dave, but everyone called him Seve. I knew both boys very well. Seve was a good friend of mine, and Dave was the cheapest SOB I ever met. He made his wife buy her own drinks out of her money, and he bought his out of his money. Strange situation, I thought. I waited for a few minutes to let things calm down. I said to Seve, "Can I see you for a minute in the utility room?" He must have thought I was going to give him hell. When he came into the utility room,

I closed the door, looked at him, and started to laugh. I said, "What the hell just happened out there?"

Seve said, "He took a swing at me, so I threw him on the ground." We both laughed our asses off because neither one of us liked Dave.

You get a variety of characters in a bowling alley. One in particular was Bruce. He lived about two miles away, on Rich Hill Road. No matter what the subject was, he was the best at it, especially after several adult beverages. One day he pulled into the parking lot in a Corvette that looked like he got it in a junkyard. I said, "Did you buy that, or did someone give it to you?"

He said, "I'm going to fix it up. I'm a good body man."

Naturally, I thought.

Another day he came in and said, "You own this bowling alley. I'll bet I can beat you in a game for five bucks."

I laughed and said, "I can beat you with one finger in the ball." He didn't know that when I was working on a pinsetter, I grabbed an eight-pound ball with small finger holes to throw to make sure it was working. I only used one finger. I actually got pretty good doing it.

Well, that must have pissed him off because he insisted we bowl a game. So I turned a lane on, and we bowled. I ended up bowling a 192 to his 127. He said, "I don't believe you beat me with one finger," and tried to pay me, but naturally I wouldn't take his money.

Another oddball was a guy named Chuck. He was the type of customer no business owner likes to see walk through the door. He complained about everything. One night he came in and must have bowled really bad. I was sitting in front of the Pepsi machine that had a TV on top of it, watching a Pittsburgh Pirates baseball game. Down the steps he came, complaining about the terrible lane conditions—the pole between lanes 4 and 5, the low ceiling height, the noise from this lounge where we had a group playing. He said, "If this continues, I'm going back to the lanes where I came from."

Well, I'd had enough of his bullshit. I jumped up from my chair and said, "Can I have that in writing?" He must have known I was pissed because after that he was as nice as pie.

Then on the other hand, you get customers who are as good as gold. Joe was that kind of customer, always polite, smiling, and courteous. He was always neat in appearance, with never a hair out of place. He drove a Buick Riviera and lived in a house trailer, which I'd been told by a girlfriend of his was spotless. One day he came in to practice with his new ball, called a Columbia Yellow Dot. It was the newest polyester ball on the market. We had just finished some major construction on the pinsetters, which sometimes could cause problems. It involved an apparatus called an accelerator, a small rubber tire driven by a motor and V-belt to get the ball back to the bowler quicker. When Joe threw his ball, it somehow jumped off the ball track and became lodged on a sharp edge on the pinsetter. Somehow the rubber tire began spinning the ball at a high rate of speed against the sharp edge, causing severe damage. When Joe yelled to me, "Ball return on eleven!" I ran down the runway and immediately smelled something wasn't right. When I got to the pinsetter, I said to myself, Holy shit. I turned the machine off. Plastic shavings were everywhere. The ball looked like it had been put in a lathe and was grooved with a gouge an eighth of an inch deep; there were scrapings around the entire surface of the ball.

I pulled the ball out of the machine and returned to tell Joe the bad news. I said, "Your ball is damaged beyond repair."

He said, "What the f**k happened to it?" with language he wouldn't normally use.

I said, "It jumped off the ball track and got stuck."

He said, "I paid sixty bucks for that ball. I want to see it."

I said, "We'll get you a new one."

Once again he said, "I want to see my ball."

I said, "OK, I'll send it back up the ball return," and returned to the pit to turn the machine back on. I wasn't out of the pit yet when I heard him say, "Holy f**k." Fortunately he was the only customer in the place at that time, and no one else heard that language.

Two days later Bobby stopped at our supplier and got Joe another Columbia Yellow Dot. I drilled the ball exactly like his previous ball, and we notified him to come in and try it out. When Joe came in, we put him on a different lane to try out his new ball. After a game and a half, I said to my father-in-law, "Do you want to have some fun?"

He looked at me over his glasses. He knew I was up to no good and said, "What are you going to do?"

I said, "I saved his ball back in the pit. I'll send the old ball back when he throws the new one."

He rolled his eyes as if to say "Are you really going to do this?"

I nonchalantly walked into the pit, waited one or two frames, then pulled his new ball out of the pinsetter and put the old ball back in. I hurried out the back door and ran to the front entrance before his ball was returned. When he saw his brand-new ball was damaged just like the old one, he became very hostile. He approached the counter and slammed the ball down and said, "What the f**k is going on?"

I started to laugh, but he failed to see the humor in my prank. He started calling me every profane word under the sun. I think he even invented some new swear words. By now even my father-in-law was holding his belly from laughing so hard. I said, "Joe, calm down," and I proceeded to tell him what I'd done. When he finished bowling, he put his new ball in his locker, headed for the door, stopped, and turned around and smiled at me. I was relieved to know he wasn't mad at me.

Next came the Tuesday-morning early birds' league, a group of housewives of various mixtures. Some were old, some young, forming a well-rounded ethnic bunch of ladies, including several Italians, Russians, Germans, and Poles. Phyliss was a very petite blonde who lived in the housing plan across the street from the lanes. She was always very neat about herself. One morning she pointed her finger at me and motioned for me to come to her. She called it her Polish magnet. She said when she wanted her husband to do something, she pointed at him in the same manner. When I got to Phyliss, I said, "What's up?"

She said, "I see you replaced the masking units."

I said, "Yes, we do that from time to time to give the place a different look."

She said, "But the old ones had a red X when we threw a strike. These ones don't have a red X. How do we know when we throw a strike?"

I thought, Polish, blonde, her maiden name ended in *ski*—that's all I'm going to say about that!

Next came Connie, an elderly Italian woman who was very bubbly and always singing and dancing around—just an all-around fun person to be with. One morning she seemed to be not herself. I saw her headed toward the ladies' room. When I saw her come out, she was walking at an unusual pace. I said, "Connie, are you OK?"

She looked at me and said, "I have to go home. I dirtied myself." I felt so sorry for her I helped putting her coat on and carried her ball out to her car for her.

Late in the afternoon one day, curious to hear a helicopter, I walked toward the door. The sound was getting increasingly loud; it sounded like the helicopter was going to land in the parking lot. As I exited through the door, I was amazed to see the helicopter flying almost at treetop level, and I could see the pilot. Next a police car came racing into the parking lot, down behind the lanes and up the other side. I asked myself what the heck was going on. I went back into the lanes to listen to my police scanner, where I learned they were looking for an escapee from the police department. The area behind the lanes was a valley between two hills that led right to the police department where he'd escaped from. As I listened to the scanner, they gave a description of the escapee: blue jeans, gray ball cap, red shirt with lettering that said "Rehab is for quitters." As I listened to the chase, the helicopter pilot radioed that he'd lost sight of the fugitive behind a neighbor's house just down the road from the lanes. I know that area very well; it had several tree stands for hunting. Was he hiding under one of them, or had he entered a house to possibly arm himself? I wondered. Now I was getting a little nervous myself. Should I go down to the house to arm myself just in case he came into the lanes? He was only a couple of hundred yards away. I cautioned the other employees and customers in the lounge to be on the lookout for him. I decided that for my own protection, I'd better arm myself—after all, I was licensed to carry a firearm.

As I headed for the house, I heard the receiver of the pay phone by the door being slammed down. I said, "Hey, bud, that phone is out of order. If you need to make a call, maybe someone in the lounge will let you use their phone." He followed me into the lounge, and I said, "Hey, folks, this guy needs to make a phone call. Can he borrow someone's phone?"

It just so happened that an Allegheny County sheriff's deputy, Jerry, was off duty in the lounge. He lived right across the street. He spoke up and said, "He can use my phone."

I took a step backward and pointed toward the kid and mouthed, "It's him." I hurried down to the lanes and called 911.

The operator went through the regular protocol: "What's your emergency, what county, what address?"

I said, "The kid the police are looking for is in Deer Lakes Lounge." I no sooner got that out of my mouth than here came Jerry and the kid out of the lounge and into the bowl.

The operator asked, "Is he in the lounge now?"

I said, "In the bowl now."

Jerry kept him very close and walked him to the door, where they were met by several policemen—even a K-9 unit. The rest of the evening went as usual until around eleven o'clock, when the door opened, and here came a local newsman named David, followed by a cameraman. I was interviewed by David, and my dusty scanner was on the noon news the next day. I found out later that this boy had stolen all his grandmother's appliances, sold them, then stolen her car. He almost hit children getting off a school bus and failed to stop for another school bus's red flashing light before wrecking the car. I was told he'd escaped from the police by telling them he had to go to the bathroom, then he bolted out a side door into the woods.

Karaoke was always good for drawing a nice crowd in the lounge, although some of the bowlers didn't like it, especially Chuck, but he complained about everything. "How can we concentrate on bowling with all that noise?" he said. Anyway, while karaoke was going on, someone came running down to the counter, yelling, "Some guy is passed out in the parking lot with his foot to the floor on the accelerator!"

I better check this out in a hurry, I thought. As I entered the kitchen area to look out the door, I could already hear the engine racing. When I opened the door, I saw smoke coming from under the hood and could hear popping noises from the engine. I knew the engine was about to burst into flames. Once again my firefighting training kicked into high gear. I grabbed the fire extinguisher from the wall and headed for the car. I don't remember doing it, but my neighbor said I broke out the window on the rear door with the fire extinguisher, reached in to unlock the front door, and pulled the hood latch while someone else got the man out of the car. When I opened the hood, the engine burst into flames, which I quickly extinguished. By now here came the fire trucks and police cars. When I reentered through the kitchen door, I could see the guy sitting on a chair in the lounge. Apparently someone knew and called his mother to come and get him. When his mom came into the lounge, she smacked him a good one upside the head and started bitching him out. I never did find out who he was or where he came from.

We had a traveling league that bowled late on a Wednesday night, after the earlier ladies' league. I was having trouble with the ball lift on the approach on lanes 11 and 12 when the ladies bowled. So I figured I'd work on it while the men bowled later. It would be one less thing for me to do the next day. The men were bowling on lanes 19 and 20, the only lanes being bowled on at that time, when all of a sudden, I heard a horribly loud thud, followed by a boisterous, loud "What the hell was that?" As I approached them to see what had just happened, all three brothers said in unison, "The ball stopped."

I knew these three very well—Cliff, Bill, and Fred—so I knew they weren't just jagging me. I said, "What happened?" They proceeded to tell me a member from the opposing team threw his ball as usual, and when it hit the pins, it just stopped. I looked down the lane, and sure enough the ball was sitting in front of the pins on lane 19. I had to manually go down the lane and send it back in the subway ball return. As I picked the ball up to send it back, I thought, That had to be a fifteen- or sixteen-pound ball. How could that have happened? The only theory I could come up with was that the pins had to have gotten wedged end to end on both sides of the ball between both kickbacks—an extremely unusual occurrence.

Summertime was when I did a lot of preventive maintenance. Lane 9 was notorious for its ball return problems. I was trying to correct that problem back in the pit area when lane 10 suddenly came on. I didn't think much of it and kept working on lane 9. When I thought I had it fixed, I went up to throw some balls to make sure. That was when I saw John, a good friend of mine, and said, "What brings you in here on such a beautiful day?"

He replied, "I've been struggling with my game lately and decided to practice for a while."

I grabbed an eight-pound ball off the rack and began throwing it on lane 9. I was not watching the pins fall; I was only concerned about the ball returning, throwing it time after time and talking to John about hunting, fishing, and whatever else came to mind. The next thing I knew, John started changing his shoes. I said, "What are you doing? I thought you were going to practice."

He said, "Joey, you pissed me off."

I was dumbfounded and said, "What did I do?"

He said, "I'm struggling to throw 190 games, and you came out of the pit with greasy hands, shorts, wearing tennis shoes, throwing an eight-pound ball with one finger, and you throw a five-bagger"—meaning five strikes in a row!

The very next day, John's brother Donnie stopped in at the lanes carrying his two-year-old son. As Donnie stood his son down, I noticed his son had his eyes fixed on the crane machine, a vending machine designed to pick up toys and drop them into a compartment protected by a wooden door. Donnie said to me, "I heard you showed Johnnie how to throw a five-bagger using an eight-pound ball with one finger."

I said, "I wasn't watching the pins fall. I was just seeing if the ball was going to return properly." We both laughed.

The next thing I heard was a bloodcurdling scream coming from Donnie's son. He had apparently put his arm into the compartment to get a toy and gotten it stuck in there. We tried frantically to get his arm out, but to no avail. I called Rick, our vending machine guy, to see if he wanted me to take the machine apart to free his arm, but Rick said, "That door is pretty tricky to prevent theft. I'll be right down." Rick only lived about a mile away, but it seemed like forever until he got there. While Donnie tried to comfort his son, Rick dismantled the machine, freed his arm, and gave him any toy he wanted.

In the thirty-seven years I owned the bowling lanes, I only got hit by a bowling ball once. It was on a Sunday night when a new bowler was joining the league. We always gave them a ten-minute practice session before beginning league play. A pin slid off spot, and the rake came down and stopped—just as it is designed to do. As I was standing in front of the rake to fix it, he threw his ball, even though the rake was down. Lucky for me, I was standing on my tiptoes when the ball hit the heels of my shoes, or it would have probably broken both my ankles.

As I came out of the pit, one of the regular bowlers said, "Aren't you going to say something to him?"

I said, "Did you see his belt buckle?" He had a marijuana belt buckle on—he was probably higher than a kite.

Helen was another senior citizen who bowled at our place. One day she came in and went to the cigarette machine to buy a pack of cigarettes. She had trouble with the machine because the pack that she wanted was sold out. She hit the coin return and got her money back. The next week she came in and said, "You stole money off of me last week."

I said, "No, I didn't, Helen. You went to buy cigarettes, and the machine was out of your brand."

She said, "I don't buy my cigarettes here."

I said, "You tried to buy them here last week."

So Helen told her husband I'd tried to steal her money last week. Well, Helen was about four feet eight inches tall, with dementia or Alzheimer's or whatever that disease is that's attacking our senior citizens.

Her husband was about the same size and build. He approached me and said, "My wife said you stole money off of her last week."

I said, "No, I didn't," and told him what she did.

He said, "I have a notion to punch you right in the nose." I'm six feet three inches tall, and he was about four feet ten inches tall. I almost said, "Do you want me to get you a stool to stand on?" but I was always taught to respect my elders.

When you own a restaurant in Pennsylvania, you have to abide by the rules of the Pennsylvania Department of Health. At least once or twice a year, you get inspected to make sure everything is up to their standards. Our inspectors were from the Allegheny County Health Department. One morning a lady came in to inspect, and she had a young girl with her as a trainee. They always start the inspection in the restrooms. Everything was fine in there, so then they went to the bar area. All was good there also. Then they went to the kitchen area and checked the walk-in cooler, freezers, and refrigerators—so far so good. Then they checked the ice machine, where she found the ice scooper inside. She said, "That scooper is supposed to be kept outside the machine."

Well, I must have been having a bad day because I snapped back at her, "You mean it's more sanitary to keep it outside the machine where a fly could defecate on it?"

That must have pissed her off because she started searching for something to write us up for. Down on her knees with a flashlight, she looked under prep tables and checked filters, fryers, grills, everything, until she spotted a dead fly on the windowsill. "I'm going to have to cite you for that dead fly." Now she had my blood ready to boil, and when she wrote up the citation, she stated that there were "dead insects on the windowsill." Insects, plural—there was only one fly! As I read the citation, I brought it to her attention. She grabbed the paper from my hands and quickly scratched out the s, making it singular. Then she spotted my dog, a black Labrador, Cubby, lying in the bowling alley section. She was well trained with all the normal commands: *sit, stay, paw, heel,* and oh yes, *protection.* The lady asked me if she came into the restaurant area, to which I replied, "No, but she is trained in protection. Would you like a demonstration?"

"No," she emphatically replied. And out the door she went.

In the mid-1970s there was a popular song out about naked people running through grocery stores, car washes, and gymnasiums—it was called "The Streak." On a Wednesday evening, we had a women's league bowling on the lower section—lanes 9-20. I was not home at the time, but when I got home, my wife said, "We got 'streaked.'"

I said, "What are you talking about?"

She said, "Someone ran naked across the twelve lanes downstairs."

I said, "In front of all the women?"

She said, "Yes, wearing a gorilla mask so no one would recognize him."

I said, "How did he get in there when both pit doors are locked?"

She said, "Someone had to have left him in."

No one seemed to know anything about it. He apparently stepped onto lane 9, ran to lane 15, stopped and shook his anatomy at the ladies, and continued on to lane 20, dodging bowling balls all the way. Someone said he had a very distinctive laugh. I think I know who it was, but I'll never tell.

Around one of the holidays—maybe Easter—we had three college students home for Easter break. They were all of legal age to drink and seemed like nice young boys. After they were in there for a while, the bartender came to me and said, "You might want to check out the men's room. I just heard a loud bang in there." When I entered the men's room, I saw where someone had punched a hole in the wall right above the urinal. I went out to look to see who all was in there—only the three young boys. Not even ten minutes later, the bartender came to me again and said, "I just heard another loud bang from in there." I checked it out, and sure enough, there was another hole in another wall. I sat out in the lanes watching to see the third one go into the men's room. As he entered the men's room, I wasn't far behind him.

As he stood at the urinal relieving himself, he turned his head and said, "I feel like I'm being watched."

I said, "Before you three guys came in here, there were no holes in the walls. I don't want another hole in this wall." I pointed to the wall behind him, and I left the men's room. About two or three minutes later, I reentered the bar to check things out. There were three almost-full glasses of beer on the bar, along with all their money left behind. I asked the bartender, "Where did those three go?" He said they'd left there in a hurry. As I reentered the men's room to look for any more damage, I couldn't see anything immediately. Then I saw on the third wall a perfect impression of knuckle prints where he'd tried to punch a hole. It turned out that wall was plasterboard glued onto a cement block wall. The knuckle prints are still on that wall even to this day.

A small group of ladies bowled on a Wednesday morning. They didn't keep averages or team standings; they just got together and bowled. Sue was one of these ladies. She was very wealthy, but she never put on a show as such. Her husband was the director and CEO of one of the local hospitals. One morning, before our regular business hours, she came in, and I sensed she was troubled by something. She said, "Put me where I won't be bothering anyone else."

I said, "Sue, you're the only one in here! Where would you like to go?"

She said, "Put me on lane 20," so I did.

As I watched her change her shoes and get her ball out of her bag, I could see she just wasn't herself. As she started to bowl, she was throwing her ball so hard she was almost losing her balance. She bowled four or five frames, sat down at the score table, and began literally talking to herself. I casually watched her before approaching her and saying, "Are you OK?"

She said, "Just leave me alone for a while."

I backed off for a while and went on about my business until she said, "I'm sorry about being so mopey, but I've got a problem."

I said, "Sue, sometimes I'm a good listener."

She said, "Sit down here, and I'll tell you what's going on." She started out by saying, "My son is a drug addict. We have spent thousands of dollars on rehab and trying to get him straightened out, but he just keeps on doing it. We just don't know what to do."

I butted in and said, "Why don't you try to find out who his supplier is and turn him in to the police?"

She said, "We did that. He just finds it somewhere else."

I asked, "Where does he get his money?"

She said, "He's stolen my jewelry and my husband's car—we never did find that. We just don't know what else to do."

I said, "Sue, I trap shoot with a man who works undercover with the narcotics squad. I'll talk to him to see if he will give me any help in your situation."

The following Monday night, at the shoot, I talked to him, and he said, "There is so much of that junk out there undermining the youth of our nation. It's very difficult to handle each individual case." To this day I've never seen Sue again.

I could be wrong, but it seems that in every neighborhood, there's always one neighbor whom nobody gets along with. We have that one neighbor. He complains about everything everyone does around him. But it's OK if he does something to other people. He has two large dogs that run free on his property and wander onto his neighbors' property to do their business. He used to bring them into the parking lot of the lanes, and they would do their business there, and he would just walk away from it, leaving it for my customers to drive through and walk through. We put a stop to that! Then one day he was trying to get his antique car running. He was dumping raw gas into the carburetor. My daughter and I were digging up worms in the garden to go fishing. I heard the car backfiring. I said to Diane, "Is it on fire yet?"

"No," she replied.

Once again he poured the gas in, and once again it backfired. I repeated, "Is it on fire yet?"

"No," she said. The third time he poured the gas in when it backfired, she said, "It is now, Dad." He grabbed a handful of sand and was going to put the fire out with that. If he would have gotten the sand in the carburetor, he would have had to take the engine completely apart.

One Sunday afternoon I decided to repair two burned-out fluorescent lights in our sign in front of the business. I only had a sixteen-foot ladder, and the sign was up twenty feet in the air. I decided to get the dump truck I was driving at the time while working in construction. I backed the truck underneath the sign and put the ladder up in the bed of the truck to reach the sign. Up the ladder I went carrying two fluorescent light tubes. The next thing I saw was my nebby neighbor coming down the road with his camera in hand, and he began taking pictures of me up on the ladder. I said, "What are you doing?"

His reply was "I'm taking pictures for the insurance company in case they want to know how you got hurt." What business was it of his?

Next we had live music out on the new patio. Here came the police! Guess who called them. There were four or five of our other neighbors sitting on the patio, eating, drinking, and having an enjoyable evening out. No driving—they could all walk home. No DUI. The police checked the noise levels—we were well within the township limits. Then for our New Year's Eve party, he called the police and said he heard we were having an underage drinking party. We've been doing New Year's Eve parties for twenty-plus years, and they have always been family oriented. There was very little drinking, and everyone was home by midnight to celebrate the new year. We found out that the police told him the next time he called to complain about us, he would be hit with a harassment lawsuit.

The phone rang, and I answered it as usual with "Deer Lakes Bowl." It was my wife. I said, "What's up?"

She said, "I need to talk to you. I'm coming up to the lanes."

While she was on her way up to the lanes, a dozen thoughts ran through my mind. Had she caught me doing something I shouldn't have been doing? Had someone died? Had she wrecked the car? And so on. When she got up to the lanes, she had a look on her face I had never seen before. I said, "What's up?"

She said, "I just got a call from my girlfriend. She has a problem."

I said, "What's her problem?" I jokingly said, "Is she pregnant? I never had sex with her."

She said, "Worse than that—her brother is in jail."

I said, "For what?" I knew he was in law enforcement.

"He apparently got too friendly with his female coworkers," she replied.

I said, "So how can I help?"

She said, "The only way to get him out of jail is a work release program. Do you think you can give him a job?"

I thought for a second, knowing he had held a pro bowler's card for a while—he was very knowledgeable about the game. He might be able to help us here. And Lord knows, maybe I could get a few hours out of this place for some rest. I said, "Go ahead and start filling out the paperwork. We'll go from there."

A week went by, and here he came through the door, shaking my hand, thanking me a dozen times for getting him out of the gray-bar hotel. He was a good person to have around—polite with the customers, always cleaning up after league bowlers, even doing some work in the ball-drilling room. One day the bartender didn't show up for work, so I asked him if he wanted to fill in at that job. He said, "Anything is better than going back to jail."

A week went by, and we started noticing the bar register was coming up short of cash. I called him and said, "Your register has been short the last two or three days in a row. Do you know why?"

He said, "I probably got you for two or three pitchers of beer yesterday also."

I thought, That's the worst case of gratitude I ever heard of—got him out of jail, gave him a job, and then he turns around and steals from me. That ended his bartending career with us, but being kindhearted as I am, I kept him working in the lanes.

One night I was working on a pinsetter, and he called me on the intercom and said, "You better come up here right away." Not knowing what had happened, I hurried out of the pit up toward the counter area, where I saw someone lying on the floor. I couldn't see immediately who it was but found out quickly it was his nephew Ryan. He had apparently overdosed on something and invited all his friends to watch.

I said, "Did you call an ambulance?"

He said, "They're on the way. I checked to see if he's still breathing. They'll give him some Narcan, and he'll throw up." It sounded like the voice of experience to me. Ryan was an exceptional athlete—he excelled at whatever sport he played, including football, basketball, and golf. He actually eagled hole 4 at a very difficult golf course in Mercer, Pennsylvania, 545 yards long, using a driver, wedge, and putter. It was a shame the drugs took over his common sense for a while, giving him temporary residence at the gray-bar hotel. While he was incarcerated, he played basketball with Black inmates, who nicknamed him White

Lightning. Thank God he got his life together and turned out to be a good human being.

Sometime around 1978 or 1979, my wife and I were fed up with the almost-every-night family arguments. I said, "We have to do something." I suggested, "We can remodel those spare rooms along lane 1." The next day we went into that area and discussed a plan to start the procedure. Some of the rooms were already paneled and had a dropped ceiling. The floor was bare concrete; I was told it used to be a dry cleaning store at one time. It was very rough, but with help from my brothers and some other relatives, we were soon moved in.

Then one night my wife was folding laundry in our bedroom. She called me out at the lanes and said someone was looking in the bedroom window, watching her. I ran out the poolroom doors and saw a man sitting on the hillside, looking in my wife's window. I ran toward him dressed in shorts and a tank top. He took off running up East Union Road with me in hot pursuit. He didn't go far before making a right turn into the woods, which were full of a thick briar patch, with me close behind. Eight or ten yards into the jaggerbushes, he fell. I was straddled over top of him and said, "Go ahead and move, motherf***er! I'll blow your head off!"

It was pitch black in the woods; we couldn't see each other. I didn't even have a gun, but he recognized my voice. He said, "Joe, it's me." I recognized his voice. He said, "Let's get out of here and talk about this."

As we made our way out of the jaggers, I said, "What are you doing looking in my wife's window?"

He said, "I dropped my keys and was looking for them." I knew that was total bullshit. But considering who he was, I just walked away.

When I got back into the lanes, my father-in-law said, "What the hell happened to you?" I looked like I'd been in a fight with a bobcat from running through the jaggers in shorts and a tank top. He said,

"Why don't you go get cleaned up?" Just then my mother-in-law came in and wanted to know what happened.

I explained everything to her, and she said, "I'm going to call the cops."

The next thing I knew, I was sitting in a police car with a rookie police officer named Marty, giving him all the details. He said, "I'm very familiar with the suspect. We've had several confrontations with him and his brothers."

The next day Marty stopped by and said he'd visited the suspect and gotten the same story about dropping his keys. He wanted to know if I wanted to press charges. I said, "No, he's not worth me missing a day's work over."

The mobile home my in-laws were living in was beginning to show its age: the furnace needed repaired, and the hot water tank was leaking. The roof had been patched so many times it looked like a jigsaw puzzle—time to build a house. When I got my job at Westinghouse, I was eighteen years old. I was sitting in the personnel office filling out the paperwork. The receptionist said, "Do you want to join the employee savings plan?" She explained it to me, and I said yes. "Do you want to join the employee stock plan?"

I thought, Someday I may settle down, get married, and have children. That money may come in handy someday. So I said, "Why not?" I signed up for everything possible. The savings plan and stock plan were taken out of my pay every week—I never even missed it. To make a long story short, I ended up with 1,429 shares of Westinghouse stock. Now to find a construction company. We heard of a local family interested in starting their own business. We contacted them, and the ball started rolling. There were six or seven brothers, all with different skills—one carpenter, one plumber, one electrician, one plasterer, and so on. The plans were submitted to the township but once again denied. Oh no, I thought, here we go fighting the township again. The township ordinance stated that you must have fifteen feet between your building and your neighbor's property; we only had twelve feet. Then we found out if we attached the house to the bowling lanes, the house would be an addition to the lanes. No problem—a breezeway solved the problem, and construction began. My wife and I were with our kids in our apartment, and my in-laws were staying with Bobby in his spare room. The house was built under one roof but almost as a duplex—the in-laws had their own bedroom, bathroom, kitchen, and living room. My wife and I had our own bedroom, kitchen, living room, and two bathrooms, and each of our daughters had her own bedroom. There was also a game room in the basement, plus enough garage space to park three vehicles. With the house being attached to the lanes, we had easy access through a hallway door through the breezeway and into a door along lane 9. It was a perfect setup for rain or snowy weather.

One night I heard my in-laws coming in the hallway door after closing the lanes. I could tell they were fighting about something. I heard my mother-in-law say, "Why the hell did you tell them I wore falsies?" Back in the day, falsies were what is now called a padded bra. My mother-in-law had several different ways to show her shapely figure—when she was doing laundry, she made no effort to be discreet about hiding her undergarments.

Anyhow, the next morning I said to Bob, "What the hell were you fighting about last night?" Bob and I had a better relationship than just father-in-law to son-in-law. We could talk guy to guy. He proceeded to tell me that at the proprietor dinner last night, he and several other owners were gathered together, and the subject came up about his shapely wife. Bob, being the comedian as usual, said, "That's all foam rubber." Well, it didn't take long until that comment got back to my mother-in-law. Her blood must have been boiling all the way home. I'll bet he didn't have sex for a week or so.

During the summer things are pretty slow. We had to do something to get money coming in so we could make our $3,750 mortgage payment. We asked our vendor if he could bring in a pool table and an air hockey machine, maybe a video or pinball machine. No problem—we had a very good relationship with our vendor. One evening a group of students came in to play pool—some regulars and some strangers. One of the regulars ordered some food, but when he went to the restroom, the strangers ate all his food. He told Bob what happened, and Bob said, "Go order again—I'll take care of it." That was the kind of guy he was, so when the food came out, Bob was approached by one of the strangers asking for some hot sauce. Bob, being the practical joker that he was, gave him some hot sauce called Chinese hot sauce. It was so hot you could almost see smoke coming off it. Bob watched as the stranger doused a chicken wing with the Chinese hot sauce. As the hot sauce took effect, the stranger made a beeline for the water fountain downstairs, clearing all five steps but falling twice in the progress. Bob laughed until his glasses fogged up.

One of the regulars came to me and asked to use the phone, which we didn't normally allow. He said, "I need to call the police."

I said, "What's going on?"

He said, "You'll see."

Bob looked at me over his glasses. I just shook my head and said, "Something is going on. I don't know." The next thing I knew, a police officer was coming in the bowling lanes door. I looked into the poolroom, and another officer was coming in that door. I recognized him—it was Marty, the rookie police officer. He was handcuffing a tall, thin, blond-haired boy, and out the door they went. When Marty returned to retrieve the suspect's coat, the suspect disappeared. It was fifteen degrees outside, and we had gotten a fresh two inches of snow that day. Marty began tracking the suspect to a door that led to some spare rooms alongside lane 1. His tracks showed that he had backed up to try the doorknob in handcuffs. It was locked! Marty followed the tracks into the woods, where he found the suspect, who had apparently tried to jump across a ditch in handcuffs and broken his leg. Had Marty not tried to follow him, he would have frozen to death. I never did find out what he did to get himself in trouble.

For insurance reasons we had to have our fire-suppression system inspected yearly. Ivan came to inspect ours, and after checking nine fire extinguishers, he told my wife we had to redo our system over the fryers. I approached him and said, "What's wrong with it?" He said the sprinklers had to be directly over the fryers, and It would cost about $600 to change it. I looked up at the sprinkler head, slid the fryer six inches to the right, directly under the sprinkler, and said, "How's that?"

He said, "You don't want me to make any money at all today, do you?"

Damian was one of our regulars. I've watched him grow up from day one. He came in on a field trip with the sixth-grade gym class. I always took half the class, with the teacher's permission, of course, back in the pit to watch the pinsetters work while the other half bowled. Then we would switch, but I always warned them before they entered the pit to be careful because once in a while the machines would spit out a pin. Wouldn't you know it—just as Damian walked behind lane 18, it spat a pin out. He caught it in full stride and handed it to me as if it were an everyday thing.

After graduation Damian joined the armed forces. He was home on leave one afternoon and came into the lounge with his girlfriend. With our surveillance camera, I saw him sitting at the bar, so I thought I would go up to say hello. When I walked into the lounge, I went behind the bar and headed toward him to welcome him back home. He jumped off his seat and said to his girlfriend, "He's packing," meaning I was carrying a firearm. He always thought I was carrying a gun for some reason or other. I don't know where he got that idea, but he was scared to death of me.

In the thirty-seven years I owned the place, we got robbed three times. The first time was when we were under construction on the new twelve lanes on the lower section. A man entered the site with his German shepherd dog by his side. I didn't think a lot about it at the time; I thought he was just being nebby. It turned out he was casing the place to see what he could get and where he could get it. The next day, when I got home from work, Bob said, "We got robbed last night."

I said, "How do you know that?"

He said, "Someone broke into the cigarette machine."

I immediately went into the construction area where we had relocated the cigarette machine and saw that the front of the machine had been pried open with a pry bar from the tool cabinet located behind lane 4. Whoever had done it was familiar with the place, and his dog had left a deposit on the poolroom floor. He left the pry bar on top of the machine and the front of the machine open. He must have known the vending machine man was coming to fill the machine the very next day. We probably lost between $100 and $150 of cigarette money in quarters. We knew who did it, but we couldn't prove anything.

The second time we got robbed was when the poolroom had twelve to fifteen regulars, some not-so-regulars, and a few strangers. On Friday our vending machine guy came in and said to Bob, "When did you get robbed?"

Bob said, "I didn't know we did."

He said, "Come on, I'll show you." He took Bob into the poolroom and showed him how someone had pried open all the doors on the pinball and video machines and taken all the quarters, maybe $20 – $25. Nobody saw anything—imagine that. We found out later from one of our regulars that it was a kid by the name of Jessie, who later spent time in the gray-bar motel for breaking into cars, toolsheds, and houses.

The third time we got robbed was on a weekend when my wife and I were away at our campground in Mercer, Pennsylvania. When we got back home on Monday morning, my mother-in-law said, "The alarm went off in your bedroom." She stated, "I shut it off and turned it on again, and everything seemed OK." Wrong; it was not the case. I went up to the lanes and discovered that all three video poker machines had been broken into. The police were notified and soon came in to take pictures and interview my mother-in-law about the time and approximately how much money was taken. The next day the police returned and said they had caught the robber. Apparently the detectives on the case had a tracking device on the robber's car so they could catch him in the act for his next job. I found out later from one of the detectives that they were in the church parking lot right next door while he was robbing us—well, at least they caught him.

A few months went by, and here came the local police into the lanes. I thought, What the heck is going on now? They told me that the trial was coming up next week, and they wanted me to testify. I said, "I've never been to court before, but I'll be there." So the next week came, and off to court I went, to the Allegheny County Courthouse in Pittsburgh. I was nervous as hell; I'd never had to testify before. Sitting in the hallway, I was approached by a gentleman wearing a suit and tie. He said, "It's all over." I didn't recognize him right away, but he was a local police officer.

I said, "Sorry, I didn't recognize you out of uniform."

He laughed and said, "He confessed about everything. He'll be going away for a long time."

I don't remember what year it was, but the Steelers were in the playoffs. Unfortunately they lost. It must have been a full moon or something because it seemed like all the distraught Steeler fans came into the lounge. I was in the lower area running the counter when someone came to me and said, "You better get up here right away. Some kid is trying to pick a fight with everyone in here." I looked at the surveillance camera and saw a young man of slender build approaching almost every guy in the lounge, bumping into them on purpose. I thought I'd better get up there to see what his problem was.

As I entered the lounge, the bartender said, "You better get him out of here, or there is going to be a fight."

As I approached him, he looked up to my six-foot-three-inch frame and kind of backed down a bit. I looked down to his five-foot-five-inch frame and said, "I think it's time for you to leave," and started showing him toward the door. He left, but by the time I got back downstairs, he had entered the bowling lanes and started toward me. I said, "Get out of here, and don't come back!" Once again I forcibly showed him where the door was. He walked into the parking lot and continued to egg me on into a fight. Well, being a distraught Steeler fan myself, I'd had enough of his bullshit. I approached him to confront him—wrong move on my part, I guess. We began to wrestle. The next thing I knew, I was face down in the parking lot with a sizable piece of my hair missing, which I found the next day on a corner of a railroad tie wall. I was told that five-foot-five-inch man had been a star wrestler on the high school wrestling team a few years ago, and he was using that strength-enhancing drug called fentanyl. No wonder he kicked my butt.

After the second time we got robbed, we decided to get a burglar alarm installed. We called an alarm company in New Kensington, Pennsylvania. They sent a worker named Emil to install the alarm, and two days later we were secure. A new season was right around the corner, and we were gaining a lot more business. With Bobby pursuing his nursing career and me at Westinghouse, that left Bob the difficult job of lane conditioning every day. That included dusting caps and gutters every day and using a bug sprayer to oil the lanes. Needless to say, that was a lot of walking for a veteran with a bad knee from a service-related injury. Not only that, but while he was working on the lanes, he couldn't get to the phone in time for the numerous phone calls per day. We decided to get a new device called an extend-a-phone, a portable phone he could carry on his belt in a carrying case. It made it easier for him to get the work done while still conducting business.

This phone had many uses, including when one time, at 2:00 a.m., the alarm went off in my bedroom. I armed myself and went to investigate. I checked all the doors and windows, but there was nothing, so I went back to bed. Twenty minutes later the alarm went off again. Thinking maybe someone was in there hiding, I checked it out again. There was still nothing, so I went back to bed. The third time, twenty minutes later, I said to my wife, "I'm going to get that new phone and stand in the utility room where the alarm won't pick me up. Call when the alarm goes off again."

Sure enough, twenty minutes later she called and said, "It just went off." I stepped out of the utility room just as the furnace kicked on and saw some stars, on which we had bowlers' names and high scores hanging from the ceiling, swinging back and forth. That was the end of those stars.

In June 2004 I began to hear rumors that one of our bowlers was going to attempt to break a record in the *Guinness Book of World Records* by bowling more than fifty-five hours and sixteen minutes. The record was currently held by an Australian bowler. I kept a low profile at the event by keeping my mouth shut and my ears open. As the details mounted, I thought I could help the situation by putting in my two cents. The bowler's name was Ronnie, and I knew him very well. He was a firefighter and a marathon runner in excellent health. I found out that according to the Guinness rules, he would get a fifteen-minute break every eight hours. I said to him, "Wouldn't a shower feel great during one of your fifteen-minute breaks?"

He said, "Jo-jo"—he always called me that—"would you do that for me?"

I said, "Of course. My house is attached to the bowling alley, and you could shower there." We decided to take turns during the eight-hour shifts among ourselves—me, Bobby, Bob, and Bill, a worker. I happened to be working the midnight shift when the eight-hour break came at 2:00 a.m. We had a change of clothes and all his necessary needs laid out in the hallway shower. I was watching the clock to see when it was time to go. Guinness was there filming the entire event. I said, "Ronnie, when you throw the next ball, it's time." He delivered the next ball, and out the door we went, through the breezeway and into the house. When I opened the bathroom door, there sat my mother-in-law on the toilet. I said, "Come into my bedroom and use my shower. I'll get your clothes when my mother-in-law is done." So into my shower he went with my wife sleeping in the bed—she never even woke up.

Ronnie's herculean event started on Sunday morning and didn't end until 7:40 p.m. Tuesday. I was eating supper when my eldest daughter came down to the house and said, "You better get up there. He looks like he's had it."

When I got up to the lanes, I saw he was done. I said, "Ronnie, do you remember our agreement?" He nodded yes. Ronnie and I had agreed that if he said he was done, he was done, and if I said he was done, he was done. I saw he had enough—he'd bowled a total of 362 games over fifty-five hours and forty minutes, setting a new world record. The event was covered by all the local radio and TV stations, earning more than $5,500 as a benefit for a Parkinson's association. Money was collected from a Chinese auction and donations from local businesses.

Splits and Giggles

On Friday afternoon senior citizens were bowling, and through the door came a uniformed sheriff with paperwork in his hand, which he presented to me. He said, "You have been served," and walked away. I didn't know what he meant and put the paperwork in the office for Bob to read.

One of the senior citizens approached me and said, "Who's getting sued?"

I said, "I have no idea." Well, I found out the next day we were getting sued for a patron who had left our place and gotten killed in an automobile accident. Time passed until we were to appear in court in Pittsburgh. As my wife and I sat in our insurance's court-appointed attorney's office, he informed us we would probably lose the case because the presiding judge had been disbarred as a judge by him and sent back to juvenile detention. To make a long story short, we lost the case after nine days in court, and the settlement was $153,000. Our insurance company sued their insurance company, and the whole thing ended up at $135,000. I never did understand legal proceedings. The case ended on December 23, two days before Christmas—not a very pleasant Christmas for us.

To say our attorney was piss poor would be an understatement. He never attempted to see if the deceased was even served at our lounge or if he stopped at any of the other nine licensed establishments between our place and his destination.

In the summertime my wife and I shot trap in a traveling league consisting of five different sportsmen's clubs. You meet a varying group of individuals in that sport—accountants, doctors, scientists, truck drivers, and so on. One person was named Bruce F. Bruce proceeded to tell me he could fix any heating and air-conditioning unit ever manufactured. I told him I had an AC unit that wasn't working and asked if he would be able to take a look at it. I did most of the maintenance on all my heating and AC units until they came out with printed circuit (PC) boards. I was never taught how to repair them or even troubleshoot them. He agreed to come out the following week. I took him up on the roof and showed him which one of the five units wasn't working. After two and a half hours, he came down off the roof and said, "I had to tear the unit completely apart, and I can't find the problem. I'll order a new PC board to see if that's it." That was on a Thursday. We had three days of torrential rains—Friday, Saturday, and Sunday—and then the roof leaks started: one in the concourse, one in the settee area, one in the office, one on the approach area. What the hell was going on? Sixteen leaks developed almost overnight. When the rains quit on Monday, I thought I'd better get up on the roof to see what was going on. I went to the AC unit where Bruce had been working, and when I stepped on the rubber roof, I saw water squirting up through the roof. A closer examination showed a washer sticking through the roof he had apparently stepped on, putting a hole in the rubber roof.

Then came Tuesday afternoon. Bruce came through the door holding a new PC board in his hand. I said, "Bruce, you don't need that. I talked to a bowler that has an AC business last night, and he said it sounded like the thermostat was bad. He had one in his truck. He went to his truck in the parking lot, and in five minutes the AC unit was up and running."

Bruce was so apologetic. he said, "I should have checked that first." He added, "I hope you're not going to sue me because I don't have any insurance."

I said, "Relax, Bruce. I'll see you at the shoot next week."

June 3, 2009, was a date I'll remember for the rest of my life. It was a Wednesday and the night I golfed in a league in Murrysville, Pennsylvania, with a lot of the guys I knew and had gone to school with. One such guy was named Gary V., an old friend of mine and a former classmate. He was my match for that evening. I knew it was going to be a lot of fun because he was always joking around and jagging me about something or other. Gary was about six feet four inches tall and weighed about 145 pounds. He was skinny as a rail and looked like a skeleton with skin on. He had been sick with sugar diabetes all his life. He always joked about it and carried needles in his golf bag with insulin in case he needed it. He would check his level frequently and was always asking me if I wanted some. He always told me I had to watch his golf balls because the sugar had taken his eyesight so bad he couldn't follow the balls anymore. As the match went on, I started feeling like a wrung-out washrag. I wasn't feeling very good at all. Gary said, "I've been watching you. Are you feeling OK? You're not looking good at all."

I said, "All of a sudden, I feel really tired." He helped me put my clubs in the truck and offered to drive me home, but I said, "No, I'll be OK."

When I got home, my wife said, "What's wrong with you? You look like you've seen a ghost."

I said, "If I feel this way tomorrow, I'm going up to the medical center."

The next morning came, and I wasn't feeling any better. I called the clinic and asked if they had any openings. They said, "No, we're booked full right now. Who is this?"

I said, "It's Joe from down at the bowling alley."

There was a ten-second pause, then she said, "How fast can you be here?"

I said, "Five minutes."

She said, "Get up here ASAP."

When I walked in, it was straight into a room, and the doctor was there immediately. She said, "I'm going to draw some blood, and I'll be right back." When she reentered the room, her expression was as if she were talking to a dead man. She said, "Go home, do everything you have to do, and get down to the hospital. I already have you a room."

When I got home, I said to my wife, "How soon is supper?"

She said, "Twenty minutes. Why?"
I said, "I have to get to the hospital."
She said, "I'll take you to the hospital. What's wrong?"
I said, "I guess we'll find out when we get there."

When we got to the hospital, I went straight through admissions and up in a wheelchair to a room where the cancer team was waiting. IVs and shots started immediately. I really didn't know what the heck was going on. Later that evening I was visited by two doctors from the clinic and two cancer doctors, who informed me that I had chronic lymphocytic leukemia. They proceed to tell me that it was treatable. If I'd had the other type, which is acute lymphocytic leukemia, I would only have had six months to live. The treatments continued for my nineteen-day hospital stay, with shots in my stomach three times a day and several chemo treatments to follow. And now, fourteen years later, I'm able to write this book.

In the summertime our Sunday-night bowling league turned into a drinking league that played the game of golf. The league officers located a golf course not far from the lanes, nicknamed the Ditch. It got its name because of a huge ravine between the tee box and the green on hole 4. Each week everyone would meet at the lounge in the lanes to get primed for the afternoon of golf. The ladies took turns cooking for the whole group, which meant they only had to cook one or two times on a Sunday all summer long—the ladies loved that. It was always interesting on the first tee to watch people who had never played the game try to hit a golf ball. Larry M. tried to hit his tee shot eleven times without hitting the ball. On his twelfth attempt, the ball came off the toe of his club, ricocheted into the parking lot, and ended up in the middle of the fairway. It was hilarious—the crowd roared.

Next came Kenny B. He was badly crippled up because of a stroke during a surgery. As rumor had it, he neglected to tell the anesthesiologist he was on cocaine before the surgery. He played the game of golf with one arm. Try that—it's not easy, but he did rather well at it. Kenny had other problems too. He spent time at the gray-bar hotel for embezzlement. His brother Frank was no angel either. He introduced another man's wife to cocaine, and that got both of them in trouble. I was told he spent time at the gray-bar hotel also, something about child porn, but I'm not sure. Then there was Laverne. I could never remember her right name, so I called her Shirley, from the TV show, and she always called me Jofus for some reason or other.

Shirley was my partner on one Sunday afternoon, and we came to hole 4—the infamous ditch hole. She said, "Why don't you go ahead and hit your shot? I know I can't get over the ditch."

I said, "Shirley, there is no ditch there. It's all grass." I helped her with her stance and made a few corrections to her horrible swing. I said, "Keep telling yourself there is no ditch. It's all grass."

So while she was addressing the ball, she repeated several times, "It's all grass. There is no ditch there." When she hit the ball, it went over the ditch and almost onto the green. She started yelling, hugging, and kissing me. Everyone on the golf course heard her yell, "I got over the ditch!"

The next Sunday I was in a foursome with a guy named John R. He was a fun-loving guy who liked to jack people off on a golf course. He would unstrap clubs on a cart so the clubs would fall off, put exploding balls on people's tees, and so forth. When John found out about rich guy Bob P. in the foursome behind us, he decided to have some fun. Rich guy Bob P. wore a $5,000 diamond ring while playing golf. He drove a very expensive car, but he was the cheapest SOB you ever saw. He played golf with range golf balls, which are driving range balls that have been hit thousands of times, probably frozen from lying in the field over winter, and they have red stripes on them to identify them as range balls.

When told John I'd seen Bob driving into the field to get enough balls to play for the day, he got a shit-eating grin on his face. Bob P. was in the foursome behind us; when I saw John drive into the field, I knew what he was up to. Hole 18 was an elevated green. When we were done putting out, we told everyone in the clubhouse to come watch when Bob P. got on the green. John had put between twenty and twenty-five range balls with red stripes on them on the green. When Bob P. got on the green, he said, "How in the hell do I know which one is mine?"

    June 23, 1995, is another day I'll remember for the rest of my life. I was cutting grass on a riding lawn mower, and I stopped underneath what used to be a mulberry bush but had turned into a mulberry tree. I had already eaten the sweet berries off the lower limbs, so I decided to step up on the mower's seat to get to the higher limbs. Suddenly my youngest daughter, Dana, came running around the corner, screaming, "Dad, Pappy just died! We have to go to the hospital to sign some papers!" My wife and mother-in-law were not home, and Bobby was at work, so off we went to University of Pittsburgh Medical Center.

    When we got to the nurses' station, the formalities were taken care of, and Dana insisted on seeing Pap one more time. I said, "Dana, when people die, they don't look the same as they did when they were alive."

    She said, "I don't care. I want to see Pap again." So we went back to the nurses' station, then were escorted into the room to see Pap. Diane didn't want to go in. When Dana saw Pap, she was visibly shaken. I was glad I'd warned her. Head tilted back, mouth wide open, no teeth in his mouth—he looked like he'd fought to the end. The attending nurse said he got up to go to the bathroom, tore off his oxygen mask, and fell over dead. Needless to say, it was a tearful ride home for the three of us.

    What is it about some parents when they bring their children to a bowling center? Do they think they're coming to an amusement park, or gymnasium, or someplace where adult supervision is no longer required, like a playground? One such lady came through the door holding a newborn child, along with two older siblings, about four or five years old. She explained to me that she was going to hang out there until her husband got home from work, and he and the two older boys were going to bowl. No problem—I put them up on lane 3, where they would be out of the way of a senior citizens' league coming in. The next thing I heard was balls being thrown down lanes that weren't turned on yet. So I put a stop to that. The mother seemed to have no control over the four- and five-year-olds. I was in the kitchen, making coffee for the senior citizens' league coming in. When I came out of the kitchen, the mother was nursing her newborn and laughing at the other two boys skating out on the bowling lanes in their street shoes. She had no control over the two boys as they raced across the approach to lanes 1–8.

When people bowl in tournaments, it seems to change their personalities. One Saturday morning we were having a head-to-head tournament. We usually used lanes 9–20 for this event, but we had an unusual number of bowlers that day, so we had to use lanes 7 and 8 on the upper level. Partway through the tournament, on lanes 7 and 8, one of the guys set off the foul lights. He claimed he didn't foul. The other contestant said, "The foul lights came on, so you must have fouled." A heated argument took place, leading to one of players taking a swing at the other one. Then a wrestling match took place right on the approach. We quickly put a stop to the fight, and I explained, "We've been having trouble with those foul lights for a long time. I'll turn them off." The foul lights in those days were probably manufactured in the late 1950s. They were so outdated we replaced them when we installed the synthetic lanes.

One Monday morning we had a small ladies' league of only sixteen ladies, most of them bringing their own thermoses or containers of coffee despite our sign on the front door: "No outside food or drink permitted." After three games it seemed like their coffee all bottomed out at the same time, and they made a beeline for the ladies' room, two, three, sometimes four at a time. One of the very attractive younger ladies came out of the ladies' room with an expression on her face like she did something wrong. I said, "Gail, what's the matter?"

She looked up at me and said, "One of the toilets won't flush."

I said to myself, What kind of a mess am I going to have here? She proceeded to tell me she took the top off the tank but didn't know how to fix it. I said, "Gail, I've maintained thirteen toilets for thirty-seven years. I'll fix it when everyone leaves." The following Monday, when Gail came in, I thanked her for telling me about the toilet. I told her the stories about some of the things I've found in clogged toilets, such as combs, squirt guns, hairbrushes, and even a miniature fire truck.

After working a 40-hour week at my job, then keeping the lanes open seven days a week, I was putting in 110–120 hours of work per week. My body was starting to tell me "Enough." I had numerous back surgeries—four in all—plus elbow surgery and some others too personal to mention. We needed someone to help lighten my load. My wife and in-laws could see I was getting run into the ground. So who did we hire? Several potential names came to mind until I mentioned Donnie B. I could tell by their body language and expressions they were not in favor of my suggestion. But they agreed to give him a try. Donnie was the most dependable, honest, and dedicated employee anyone could ever ask for. He would chase pins, clean up after leagues, take out the garbage, and do anything you asked him to do. But Donnie had one major fault: he would never, never, never take a bath or shower! Time after time we asked him to clean himself up, but to no avail. Customers would complain about the way he smelled. But he would religiously show up for work.

Splits and Giggles

Donnie had a younger brother and a sister named Julie. Sometimes she would come to work with him and stay until he was done. Sometimes she would come in by herself. When she did, she would always say, "Where's the dummy?" referring to Donnie. Time after time she would say, "Where's the dummy?" until one day Jim M. was standing there. When Julie came through the door and said, "Where's the dummy?" Jim M. started laughing, saying where he used to work, they had a life-size dummy. They used to scare the shit out of people by placing it in unusual places such as restrooms, closets, and so on. That started the gears turning. The next thing I knew, we were making our own life-size dummy—an old pair of blue jeans, black tennis shoes, and an old, beat-up sweatshirt got things started.

I very carefully sewed the black shoes onto the blue jeans with fishing line, then sewed the sweatshirt to the jeans so carefully you couldn't even see the stitches. We stuffed crumpled-up newspaper into the jeans and sweatshirt. He was starting to really look good. Now we needed some hands. I don't know where they came from, but someone found a pair of rubber hands that looked so real it was scary—they had veins and even fingernails. They were sewn onto the sweatshirt.

It was a little tricky, but I got it done. Now we needed something for a head. A few days went by until I heard someone yell, "Yosko!" That's "Joseph" in another language. Jimmy always called me by that name. I turned and looked. To my surprise, it was Jimmy's body but not his face. He looked like he'd aged fifty or sixty years.

I said, "Where in the hell did you get that?" He had on a rubber mask that looked so real, with eyes half open, a wart on the nose, and missing teeth. He said a buddy of his gave it to him to use for the dummy. That was perfect! So I took an old soccer ball, put it in the rubber mask, and sewed it very carefully onto the dummy's body. Now the fun began. I put our new resident dummy on a seat at the score table on lane 5. We had so much newspaper in him he would hold any position you put him in. I put his right hand under his chin as though he was thinking about something. School had just let out, and through the door came a lady with two young boys to bowl. I gave them their rental shoes and assigned them to lane 5. After a few minutes, the older of the two boys came down to the counter and said, "There is some guy sitting at our score table."

I said, "Well, just ask him to move."

The boy shook his head and said, "He's scary. Would you please ask him to move?"

So up I went to ask this guy to move. I said, "Hey, buddy, these people want to bowl here. How about moving?" There was no reply. "OK, I guess I'll have to move you." When I picked him up, the mother's mouth dropped open, and she began to laugh hysterically.

We decided our dummy needed a name, so we started referring to him as Harry. My wife told me, "We're getting a new bartender today at three o'clock. She'll probably be nervous. Let's loosen her up a bit." So back I went to get Harry from behind lane 11, where we'd been storing him. I took him out to the lounge, set him on a barstool, and wrapped his hands around an empty beer glass. At 2:45 p.m. here came the new bartender, a cute little blonde named Crissy. She approached my wife in the kitchen to see what to do first. Now my wife wanted to have some fun too. She said, "Why don't you go out and see if Harry needs another beer?"

After a minute or two, Crissy returned to the kitchen and said to my wife, "I asked him three times, and he won't answer me."

My wife said, "I'll take care of this." She went out to the bar, grabbed Harry off the stool, and started dancing with him. Crissy stared for a moment and didn't know whether to laugh, cry, or run out the door to get away from these crazy people.

Splits and Giggles

The next episode with Harry was when an insurance man came in to check out the place for insurance reasons. I showed him all the exits and told him where all the smoke alarms and fire extinguishers were located for him to check. When he came out of the pit for me to sign some papers, he said, "Boy, that guy back there is really grumpy."

I said, "What guy?"

He said, "That guy sitting on those boxes of bowling pins. I spoke to him two to three times, and he never even said a word."

I don't know how I kept a straight face, but I said, "There better not be anyone back there because you and I are the only ones in this building."

He said, "I'm telling you there is some guy sitting on a box of bowling pins."

I said, "Let's go see." As we walked back on the runway, he kept describing this guy to me. As we turned the corner behind lane 9, I said, "Now where is this guy?"

He said, "Right there," and pointed toward Harry.

I walked over to where Harry was sitting and said, "You mean this guy?" and punched him in the nose.

The insurance man's eyes got wide open, and he was speechless for about eight to ten seconds. Finally he said, "Wait until I tell my wife about this day."

Once again the Sunday-night drinking-bowling league came in, and I was advised there was a new couple joining the league. Ed and Susan were just starting to date. They were a very young couple, but they seemed to fit right into the league. After the second game, someone said, "Are you going to drop the dummy on Susan?" By now dropping the dummy was something we did to new bowlers in the league. It involved me climbing up on the pinsetter with Harry, stepping onto the pin deck light, and watching people through a small crack. When they threw their ball, I would drop Harry, making it look like Donnie fell off the machine. Naturally "Donnie" was involved in this. When he found out we were doing a dummy drop, he went into the pit and made it look like the pinsetter was broken down. Then I went back, got Harry, climbed up on the pinsetter, and waited for Susan to bowl. When Susan threw her ball, I made the best dummy drop ever. Her ball hit the dummy in the head, and everyone in the place yelled, "You killed Donnie!" She was so upset she ran into the ladies' room and wouldn't come out. Several of the ladies went in to tell her it was just a joke, but she refused to come out.

Eddie finally went in to coax her out, but in the meantime I brought Harry out and put him on Susan's chair, crossed his legs, and propped his head up with his hand. Eddie walked her over to her chair and said, "This is the guy you hit." She was so pissed she punched Harry, knocking him off her chair. The crowd roared.

Then came our year-end banquet. We rented a chalet at a world-famous ski resort near Donegal, Pennsylvania. Chalet is a fancy word for a large log cabin with six or eight large bedrooms and a huge hospitality room. And of course, Harry had to go with us. Our chalet was right next to the main lodge—a beautiful seven-story stone building. Harry was placed on a lawn chair right outside the front door. After the third day, two security guards approached and knocked on the front door at ten in the morning. Jeff, the president of the league, hung over from the previous night of heavy drinking, answered the door with a beer in his hand. "We received a call from a lady on the third floor that a man was dead sitting on a lawn chair. He hasn't moved for three days," said the security guard.

While the second guard was poking Harry with his nightstick, Jeff about lost it. He said, "Oh, that's Harry. He did a line of cocaine three days ago. He'll be all right." The two guards realized they had been tricked, turned around, and left.

Splits and Giggles

That afternoon it was time to go golfing. We packed up the coolers with as much beer as possible. It was a hot day, so I thought a six-pack should get me through. It turned out we found a nine-hole golf course. It was a slow play, hot day—I was out of beer on the third hole. I was in a foursome with Scott C. He said, "Drink some of mine."

I said, "I don't want to drink your beer."

He had a huge cooler, maybe two or three cases. He said, "I'll match you beer for beer." It was a wrong thing to say to me because I am a pretty good beer drinker.

After nine holes, maybe ten or twelve beers, we said, "Let's play nine more," and went to the parking lot for everyone to replenish coolers. All of a sudden, I saw a golf cart coming with Harry strapped onto the roof. Away we went to play nine more, but by now everyone, including me, was about shit-faced drunk.

When the last cart came pulling into the clubhouse with Harry on top of it, the owner and his daughter came running out, screaming, "Get that guy off the roof of that cart!" So the driver, knowing the straps had been removed, slammed on the brakes, sending Harry flying onto the ground in front of the cart, and continued to run over him. I thought the owner was going to have a heart attack.

When we got back to the lodge, I asked Scott's wife how he was doing, and she said, "We had to pour him into the van."

After dinner four of us decided to go play tennis. While playing, we could hear an unusual noise coming from the direction of the lodge. *Whaap*—the noise continued several times. The next thing we knew, water balloons were splattering on the tennis courts. Someone in our group had brought a three-man slingshot. It had two huge rubber bands connected by a pouch in the middle. It required one person on either end with a handle and one person to load the pouch and pull it back. They were shooting oranges and lemons 350–400 yards up the ski slopes. Then they decided to shoot water balloons at us playing tennis. We could hear the *whaap*. Four or five seconds later, a balloon would splatter on the tennis courts. This went on for ten or twelve minutes, then suddenly stopped. When we got back to the hospitality room, we found out the security guards had gone to Jeff's room and said if one more balloon was launched from his room, he would have to find another place to stay.

The Friday-night pin busters' league had been in existence for thirty-plus years. They'd bowled at another house before it closed and became a restaurant. A nice bunch of close-knit guys, they rarely changed personnel. But when one would pass away, they had a waiting list to join. One night Gary came to me and said, "We got a new guy. Could you drop the dummy on him?"

I said, "Gary, there's four inches of snow out there."

He said, "Can you do it or not? I need to know so I can tell the guys."

I said, "OK, but it will take me a while."

By now Harry was starting to look a lot like Donnie after being hit with a couple dozen bowling balls and run over by a golf cart, but I'd added fishing line to both wrists so I could move his arms and hands after he'd been hit. So I went out the back door by lane 9, down eight snow-covered steps, up to the door by lane 8, all while carrying a life-size dummy, and finally onto the pin deck light on 4. OK, here came the new guy bowling. When he threw his ball, I dropped Harry. The new guy hit him in the chest and knocked him into the rake. I shut the machine off and started moving his arms with the fishing line. Everyone yelled, "You hit Donnie!" The new guy ran down the middle of the lane. But when he tried to stop, the slippery lane oil made his feet go out from under him, and he landed flat on his back. He could have gotten severely injured. I thought, I better quit this nonsense before someone really gets hurt bad.

Splits and Giggles

After the untimely death of my wife, a tournament was named in her honor, called the Polly Tournament. The prize fund brought bowlers from the tristate area and more—even several pro bowlers attended. To advance to the finals, one of the bowlers left a 7–10 split in the tenth frame. He tried to throw the ball so hard he said his thumb stuck. The ball hit the ceiling and the fluorescent light fixture, breaking both eight-foot tubes all over six lanes. It took three of us over a half hour for the cleanup. Then the tournament director insisted that we recondition those six lanes. He ended up missing the cut anyhow, and another asshole was born.

In my early growing-up years, it seemed like bowling alleys were always burning down. I always wondered why. Well, back in those days, many bowling alleys were open all night long. Smoking had not yet been banned in public buildings. People would empty their ashtrays into the garbage cans, which would eventually catch fire. The lanes at that time were coated with an extremely flammable material after being resurfaced. It is my understanding that synthetic approaches were installed in a bowling center in New York. When the center caught fire, the lanes burned to the foul line and stopped at the synthetic approaches. Why not have synthetic lanes? When we bought the center in 1976, we couldn't afford an automatic lane-conditioning machine, so Bob would oil the lanes by hand with an old-fashioned bug sprayer. When he was done oiling, there would be an oily cloud that would eventually settle on everything. What a mess!

Ed and Susan had been dating for some time now and decided to get married, so through the door came Jim M., wearing a shit-eating grin on his face. I said, "What's up?"

He smiled at me and said, "Where's Harry?"

"Back in the pit. Why?"

Joseph E. Schwarzel

"We're taking him to Ed and Susan's wedding. We rented a tuxedo for him, and we need to get his shoes polished and get him cleaned up a bit." So off went Harry to a wedding. Someone with a camcorder even recorded him doing the bunny hop. Back in the days of wooden lanes with only black rubber balls, the heads of the lanes just beyond the foul line would turn black from the black rubber bowling balls. Someone decided to coat that area with oil to eliminate that problem. It worked so well that they experimented with putting a path of oil down the lane, thus making it a blocked illegal lane. Back in those days, if someone threw a 300 game, it was on the eleven o'clock news. That pair of lanes had to be shut down, and you had to box up the pins until someone from American Bowling Congress came out to check the lanes and weigh the pins to make sure everything was legal. To get a 300 ring in those days was very prestigious.

ACKNOWLEDGMENTS

I'm going to dedicate the writing of this book to my wife, Polly, to whom I was married for forty-two wonderful years. We did everything together: bowling, golfing, trap shooting, Ping-Pong, camping; she was very competitive at whatever she did. She didn't like to lose. Her accomplishments in the game of bowling are way too many to cover, but I will mention a few: She won a color TV in the early 1970s in Channel 4's women's championship bowling, plus three automobiles. She gave one to her brother, traded another for a truck to plow snow at the lanes, and kept one for ourselves. She also held the world record for the highest three-game series ever bowled by a woman. She bowled 266-298-277 for an 841 series, and she was seven and a half months pregnant with our youngest daughter. She was inducted into the Greater Pittsburgh Bowling Hall of Fame in 1988 and the Pennsylvania State USBC Hall of Fame in 2016. She also won the nationals in singles in 1985 with a 694 series, but unfortunately her life was cut short by a massive heart attack on January 1, 2015, thirty days before her sixty-fifth birthday.